I REMEMBER PAPA

Helen Ketteman • pictures by *Greg Shed*

PUFFIN BOOKS

*For my father, Dr. Jack B. Moon, whom I miss; and
for my father-in-law, Dr. Charles H. Ketteman, with love*

H.K.

To my brother, Mark

G.S.

PUFFIN BOOKS
Published by the Penguin Group
Penguin Putnam Books for Young Readers,
345 Hudson Street, New York, New York, 10014, U.S.A.
Penguin Books Ltd., 27 Wrights Lane, London W8 5TZ, England
Penguin Books Australia Ltd., Ringwood, Victoria, Australia
Penguin Books Canada Ltd, 10 Acorn Avenue, Toronto, Ontario, Canada M4V 3B2
Penguin Books (N.Z.) Ltd, 182-190 Wairau Road, Auckland 10, New Zealand

Penguin Books Ltd., Registered Offices: Harmondsworth, Middlesex, England

First Published in the United States of America by Dial Books for Young Readers,
a division of Penguin Putnam Inc., 1998
Published by Puffin Books, a division of Penguin Putnam Books for Young Readers, 2001

1 3 5 7 9 10 8 6 4 2

Text copyright © Helen Ketteman, 1998
Pictures copyright © Greg Shed, 1998
All rights reserved

THE LIBRARY OF CONGRESS HAS CATALOGED THE DIAL EDITION AS FOLLOWS:
Ketteman, Helen.
I remember papa/ Helen Ketteman; pictures by Greg Shed.
p. cm.
Summary: After saving to buy a baseball glove, a young farm boy takes a memorable trip
to town with his father.
ISBN 0-8037-1848-9.—ISBN 0-8037-1849-7 (lib.)
[1. Fathers and sons—Fiction] I. Shed, Greg, ill. II.Title.
PZ7.K494Iam 1998 [E]—dc20 94-33173 CIP AC

Puffin Books ISBN 0-14-056607-4

Printed in the United States of America

The artwork was prepared using designer gouache on canvas.

When I was young, *I got up at daybreak every weekend*
to help Papa clean out the barn, and feed and water the horses.

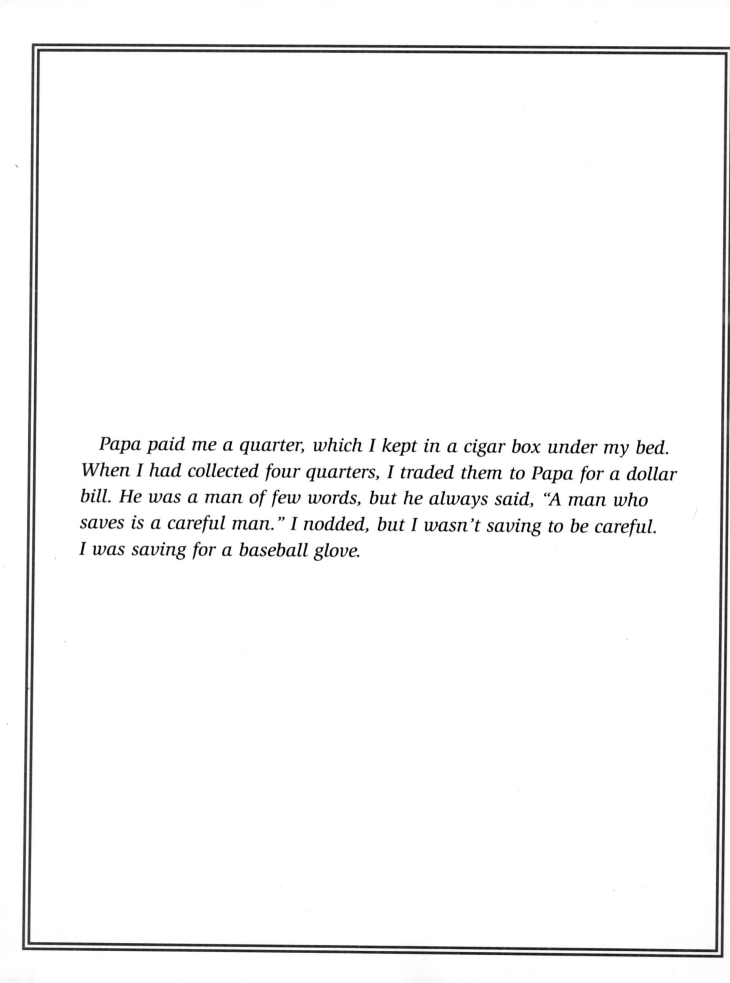

Papa paid me a quarter, which I kept in a cigar box under my bed. When I had collected four quarters, I traded them to Papa for a dollar bill. He was a man of few words, but he always said, "A man who saves is a careful man." I nodded, but I wasn't saving to be careful. I was saving for a baseball glove.

Some summer afternoons Papa found time to listen to a baseball game with me. When he turned off the radio, he always said, "One day we'll go to a game, Audie." But it seemed there was always too much work, and too little money.

Then one Saturday in midsummer Papa woke me earlier than usual....

"It's still dark outside," I complained.

Papa stood up. "Get dressed. Mama's fixing breakfast."

I pulled on my clothes and went downstairs, shivering a little in the morning cool.

Mama stirred coffee and sugar into my milk.

I ate while she made sandwiches, packing them in a paper bag like she did on school days. "Are we going somewhere?" I asked.

Mama looked at Papa and smiled. I looked at him too. He was

putting on a hat and looking at his watch. "We'd best get going if we're to make the train."

I jumped up, almost knocking my chair over. "Train? We're going on a train ride?"

Papa nodded. "My work boots are falling apart, so we're going to the city to buy new ones." His eyes twinkled, and he added, "Besides, the Reds are playing at home today, and I've put aside a little extra."

A baseball game and a train ride, all in one day! I raced back upstairs to my room to grab my baseball cap. Then I remembered my savings. Opening the cigar box, I stuffed my money into an envelope and stuck it in my pocket. Maybe we would see a glove in the city, and maybe I had enough money.

By the time we arrived at the station, the sun was coming up. The sky was pink, and yellow, and blue. Papa bought tickets, and soon I heard the clickety-clack of wheels rattling down the track.

We climbed aboard, and I pressed my nose against the window and watched the station get smaller and smaller, until it disappeared around

the curve. "How long will it take, Papa?" I asked.

"Long enough to get there," he answered.

The countryside flew past. I watched the train's reflection wiggle across the surface of the water below a bridge. We rounded a bend, and in the distance I saw the city's tall buildings.

"We're here!" I shouted as the train wheels squealed to a stop in the station. We walked to the stores, where Papa tried on work boots until he found a pair he liked. He asked the salesman to hold them until after the game.

Down the street we found a sports store. It was closed, but in the window was the most beautiful glove I had ever seen. Its golden brown leather glistened in the sunlight, and I knew it was the glove I wanted. Papa said the store would open later, and we'd check after the game. Then, while I was still dreaming about the glove, we boarded a bus for the stadium.

Soon the bus stopped, and we climbed off. I had never seen so many people in one place! Papa bought tickets, and we squeezed through the crowd and hurried to our seats.

The air smelled like hot dogs and onions, and the field had the greenest grass I'd ever seen. The dirt was raked around the bases, which

gleamed so white in the sunlight, it almost hurt my eyes to look at them. On the sidelines, players played catch and swung bats.

When the umpire yelled, "Play ball!" people clapped and whistled and cheered as the players took the field. Then, over the speaker a voice announced, "Hey! Hey! It's a great day for baseball!"

While we ate Mama's sandwiches and drank root beers, a player hit a foul ball right over our heads. We jumped to our feet, screaming with the rest of the crowd. I watched as a boy caught the ball in his glove, and wished it had been me.

During the seventh-inning stretch we went to the bathroom. On the way back to the seats I pulled Papa over to a souvenir stand. I looked at a package of baseball cards, but was afraid to spend anything. If I did, I might not have enough for the glove. I patted my pocket. It was empty!

For a moment Papa looked angry, but he took me back to the bathroom. We searched everywhere, even in the trash cans. No envelope. I slumped against the bathroom wall, and though I squeezed my eyes tight, tears trickled out the corners.

Papa dampened his handkerchief and washed my face. "Maybe someone will find it and turn it in," he said. "We'll check after the game."

I tried to enjoy the last two innings, but could think of only one thing. When the game was over, Papa spoke to the lady at the lost-and-found window. She shook her head and looked at me sadly.

I felt a huge lump in my throat. I thought Papa would be angry at me for being careless and losing my money, but he didn't say a word. Instead he took my hand as we boarded the bus.

When we got off, rather than going to the shoe store, Papa led me into the sports store. "My son wants to see the glove in the window," he said to the salesman. His voice sounded gruff, and I knew he was going to teach me a lesson about being careful with my money.

The salesman handed me the glove, and I stared at it, waiting for Papa to speak. When he didn't, I looked up. Papa was handing the salesman money.

"No, Papa!" I shouted. "That money is for your boots!"

Papa shrugged. "We have glue. You can help me repair them. They'll do for a while longer."

I looked at his face. His mouth was set in a tight line, and I knew it was useless to argue. I tried to thank him, but my voice wouldn't work anymore. Papa patted my back, and we headed for the train station.

I wore my glove all the way home. I punched my fist into the pocket a thousand times, and ran my fingers over the laces, and smelled the leather.

By the time we arrived home, the sun was setting, and the sky was

pink, and yellow, and blue. In the twilight Papa and I played catch, like
the players at the game. When it got too dark to see the ball, we went in
the kitchen and glued Papa's boots together, then set them on the porch
to dry.

Before I went to bed, I wrote the price of the glove on a piece of paper and put it in my cigar box. That night while Papa and Mama slept, I sneaked downstairs and polished Papa's old boots until they sparkled like new. In the morning Papa smiled when he pulled them on, and I could tell he was pleased.

For many Saturdays afterward, instead of taking a quarter, I had Papa help me subtract it from my balance, until I had repaid him. Papa's been gone for some years now, but I still have the glove, and I remember.